SOLDIER UNDER THE MISTLETOE

SNOWBOUND IN SAWYER CREEK

LACY WILLIAMS

CHAPTER 1

"HOLY MISTLETOE."

Mallory Trudeau couldn't help but giggle at her friend Amber's awestruck expression. Around them, guests sipped from fancy glasses and waiters carried trays of goodies, but Amber seemed to notice none of that.

Mallory followed Amber's gaze to the glittering white lights glowing from the floor-to-twenty-foot-ceiling fir that her brother Cash had had hauled in to the ranch house's ballroom two weeks ago. She'd spent six hours decorating that thing and almost broke her leg falling off the ladder. Not that she'd admitted that to Cash.

"How many years has your family hosted the Christmas ball?" Amber asked, her gaze tracking around the room that had evergreen boughs and gold accents dripping from almost every surface. Amber was a transplant, had only arrived in Sawyer Creek eighteen months ago.

"My grandma threw the first Cattlemen's Association Christmas Ball forty years ago. We've held it here almost every year since."

The Double Cross was the only nearby property with an elegant ballroom built into the huge house—thanks to Grandma. It hosted few parties apart from the Christmas ball. Mallory and Cash had roller-skated across the parquet floor when they were kids.

The only Christmas they hadn't hosted the ball had been last year.

Mallory's gaze glanced off the ballroom windows. Outside, the landscape was turning into a winter wonderland. The weatherman had predicted a light dusting, but snow was falling in heavy, feathery flakes that were piling up higher than any dust she'd ever seen.

A waiter jostled Mallory's elbow, and she wobbled on the four-inch heels that were already killing her feet.

It wasn't fair, not really. The men crowding

the room were dressed in tuxedos and dress boots, their necks adorned with bolo ties—the rancher's version of a bow tie. While the women had been glammed up in dresses like the slinky, silver-and-white evening gown she'd donned for the occasion. Big hair, bright lipstick, pinchy shoes.

She'd give anything to be wearing her old jeans and barn boots, out in the barn getting a breath of cold, sweet-smelling hay. She'd spent her whole life on the Double Cross. Glamorous wasn't in her repertoire.

It was going to be tonight.

She inhaled a deep breath of overpowering cologne—a mix of every man in the vicinity—and a hint of the evergreens.

Jingle bells. She was *nervous.* She couldn't be nervous tonight. She needed to be confident. In control. Cool.

She was the boss of the Double Cross. One of them, anyway. Between her and Cash, they'd single-handedly brought the ranch back from near-failure. Well, they were almost back to the black. She'd driven big rigs of cattle to the sale barn. Balanced books and managed the supply orders for the ten-thousand-acre propriety. Managed the food for a bunkhouse full of cowhands during branding.

All of it had been necessary over the last twelve months.

She could handle the ranch.

Surely she could handle one cowboy for one night.

She intended to dazzle one Maverick Dunlop —Cash's best friend—so that he wouldn't be able to deny the chemistry between them.

He'd been in denial since she was fifteen. He'd been nineteen at the time, and maybe a bit too old for her. But eight years had been long enough for him to find someone else if he'd wanted to, right? And the years between them no longer mattered now that they were both adults. The time for distractions and denial was over.

He was only in town for the night, attending the party at Cash's request. She had maybe four hours to get him to admit there was something between them.

This Christmas, there was only one gift she wanted.

Maverick.

And she intended to treat herself.

"Ladies."

Amber jumped when a mellow voice greeted them from behind. It wasn't the right voice, so Mallory was able to marshal herself into a slow turn.

Jace Cantrell, the man Amber worked for, stood tall and handsome in a tuxedo jacket—no tie—and boots.

Amber immediately went pink.

Jace didn't seem to notice. His gaze flicked over Amber and Mallory with the same casual interest before he offered them both glasses of champagne he held in one big hand.

"You look nice tonight." His words seemed to encompass them both. As a friend of Cash's and someone Mallory had gotten to know at the cattle association meetings, his casual greeting was appropriate, and Mallory accepted it with a nod of thanks.

But Amber barely hid a wince of disappointment. Mallory knew her girlfriend had spent a pretty penny—nannies didn't have exorbitant salaries—on the red sheath she wore, hoping to catch Jace's attention. Amber held the champagne flute awkwardly and wrapped her other arm around her middle, cupping her elbow.

"Thanks for giving me the night off," Amber said softly. "Did Bo have any trouble with the sitter?"

Jace's whole demeanor softened at the mention of his son. He stopped scanning the room and looked directly at Amber for the first time. "Other than complaining for the seven-hundredth time that you are 'way more fun' than Mrs. Ritter, he was fine."

"Good." Amber nodded, the pair wearing matching looks of adoration over the five-year-old they both loved.

And then she didn't say anything else.

"The music just started," Mallory said into the silence that was rapidly becoming awkward. "You two should catch a dance."

It was a little early in the evening for dancing. Only two elderly couples had taken to the parquet dance floor as the quartet of musicians played instrumentals of Christmas favorites.

Jace blinked, not seeming to notice the way Amber's expression had lit. "I don't think so."

He raised his champagne class to salute them and excused himself.

Crestfallen, Amber turned her back to the ballroom. The tip of her nose had gone red, and tears sparkled in her eyes. "I have to give up, don't I?"

Mallory winced. "He's either really oblivious, or..." *Not interested.* But she didn't say the words. Amber had arrived in town late one night. Skittish as a wild animal. She'd shared a little with Mallory, but most of her past was a locked up tight. She'd pinned all her hopes on tonight. Sort of like Mallory had.

Mallory waved hello to an older couple who entered the ballroom. Still no sign of Maverick.

Amber sniffled mightily and blinked at the tears. "I've been waiting for him to notice my existence, but if he can't see me in *this dress...*?" Amber shook her head. "Maybe he's just too polite to tell me I'm not his type."

Mallory h'mmd She knew how her friend felt —and knew how that rejection must have stung. She'd lived it herself often enough.

She felt a prickle of awareness at the back of her neck, the fine hairs there standing to attention.

Maverick was here.

She turned slightly on her heel, sending a

cool, confident glance across the room. There he was, standing next to Cash, one hand loosely in his pants pocket. At ease with the world. Faking it. She saw his covert glance around the room, the finger he stuck in his collar. How had he snuck past her watchful eye?

Her stomach dipped when his eyes met hers from across the crowded room. The tips of her ears went hot, her pulse raced.

She didn't look away.

Instead, she let her lips spread in an inviting smile.

His eyes flicked away. His conversation with Cash continued as if nothing had happened. As if her smile had bored him.

Jingle bells.

There's no way she was giving up.

He wanted to pretend denial?

Challenge accepted.

This was going to be a magical night, if she had to make the magic herself.

MAGIC WAS IN THE AIR. Which meant Sam "Maverick" Dunlop was on high alert.

He'd spent half his twenty-six years waiting for magic to happen.

The old goats from the Cattlemen's Association seemed oblivious. They moseyed around wearing their expensive suits, fancy wives on their arms.

There were a few single women trolling for something short-term. He'd done those kind of relationships before—if you could call them that. Wake up the next morning with a boatload of regrets.

Magic existed. Just not for him.

His stomach grumbled. He'd scarfed down a sandwich on his flight earlier, but that had been hours ago. Cash had asked him to come, so he had. Cash was grieving. So was Mallory.

Without his permission, Maverick's gaze flew to Mallory. Cash's little sister.

Not so little anymore.

She was talking to some citified guy—it wasn't difficult to tell a real cowboy from a fake. She wasn't just talking, though, she was laughing. Her hand rested on the wannabe's arm, and Maverick's gut turned into a ball of solid lead.

As if she could sense his gaze, her long lashes

lifted, and her blue eyes met his. Just one look packed a punch.

He looked away.

He didn't have to look at Mallory to know where she was in the room. Never had, not since she'd been a little kid and he a mature second grader.

Mallory didn't need Christmas magic. She made her own.

And he'd always known she wasn't for him. Cash had never had to warn him off. It was just understood between them. Mallory was off-limits.

Maverick shifted his boots, his left knee shooting red-hot flares of pain.

"That bad?" Cash asked.

He never could hide anything from his best friend. Not that first black eye his dad had given him. Not this.

He shrugged. The pain had been constant in the last month.

"You skipped your pain meds today, didn't you?" his friend asked.

Maverick just grinned. Maybe it was a little more like a feral baring of his teeth than a grin. So what?

"They lay me out," he said simply. And on a night like tonight—a night when Mallory sent him a *come 'n get me* smile like she had earlier—he couldn't afford to be off his game.

Cash stared at him, and Maverick held his gaze. The truth was, he'd laid off the meds after the first day. He was too afraid to end up like his old man. He could live with pain.

He couldn't live in a drugged-out fog.

Cash got it without Maverick having to say a word. Of course, he'd been there on those nights when Maverick had run away from home, run straight to the Double Cross.

Maverick kept one eye on the falling snow. He had a plane to catch early in the morning. He had to report back to base on the twenty-sixth. Go back to his real life.

He gestured to the party crowd with his empty glass. "You got sucked in, huh? No turning back now."

Cash had always chafed at the small-town life. It'd always been his dream to get out. After college, he'd landed in Austin, ninety minutes away. He'd held a good job in the tech sector until last year when his parents had passed.

Cash rolled his shoulders under his monkey-suit jacket. "Things are settling down. Mallory and I have been talking about making a change."

Maverick nodded, his gut pitching.

The ranch was huge. A full-time job. More, even. An around-the-clock job.

He wasn't like Cash. Hadn't wanted to leave their hometown, just his home. His adolescent dreams had been made up of his old man dying and the Trudeaus adopting him.

Even after high school when he'd joined the Marines, he'd always had the Double Cross to call home.

If Cash decided to sell, Maverick would have no link to Sawyer Creek. No home.

It was crazy to feel that way. The Double Cross wasn't his home and never had been. It was Cash's home. And Mallory's. And if they wanted to sell the massive ranch, good for them.

Cash's head jerked to the side, and Maverick followed the other man's gaze to a bombshell in a black knee-length dress. Wowsa.

"Do you know who that is?" Those legs seemed to have captivated Cash, because he couldn't seem to pull his gaze away.

"No idea."

"I'm going to..." Cash's voice was already

fading away as he shouldered into the crowd, on the hunt.

"You sure he doesn't need a wingman?" Mallory's voice came from behind him, a hit to his solar plexus. He followed his training and forced the rest of the air of his lungs.

Took a deep breath. Mistake, because all he could smell was her sweet scent. No perfume. Something flowery. Her shampoo.

Seeing her up close was like touching a warhead. Dangerous. If he moved wrong, he'd get blown to smithereens.

That didn't stop his slow perusal of her. She had her ebony hair swept up behind her head, held with some kind of combs. Probably real diamonds on those. The faintest smattering of freckles was visible beneath a soft layer of makeup—not too much to detract from her natural beauty. The bow of her lips made him desperately want to taste her.

And that dress...

It fell from her shoulders in a ripple of fabric that was both white and silver and neither. A knee-high slit gave a tantalizing glimpse of shapely calf and heels that put her at the perfect height for...

He abruptly ended that train of thought, taking a slug of the too-sweet punch.

"Where's my kiss hello?" she asked.

He choked, coughing.

She was grinning up at him, the monster. She patted his bicep. "Right. Better wait until later. In private. Don't worry. I know where all the mistletoe is."

His mouth went dry. His eyes dropped to her lips. They parted slightly, and fire shot through his veins. Just one taste...

A raucous laugh from nearby broke the moment.

What was he doing?

Losing his mind, maybe.

"I thought I saw your boyfriend." He let his gaze roam over the people in their corner of the ballroom, pretending to look for the guy. "Where is good old Howie, anyway?"

Her nose wrinkled. "Howard Powers and I are friends. Nothing more. Where'd you hear about that anyway?"

He didn't answer, and she nodded because she already knew. Cash. His best friend kept him in the loop on the homefront, wasn't shy about sharing details on Mallory's life, though he couldn't know how Maverick waited with his stomach twisted in knots every time.

One of these times, Cash was going to call and say she was engaged.

"You sure he knows that?" he asked, tracking back to the current conversation.

"Very." The word was firm, with a tinge of... bitterness? Something. Enough that his instincts sat up and took notice. Had something happened with Howie?

"What about you? No girlfriend?" she asked before he could follow up.

"No." Not for a long time.

"Cash said you're only in town for the night. I'm sure he'd love it if you could stay longer. We've got plenty of bedrooms here. You could bunk down, stay through Christmas."

Imagining Mallory pulling a pile of gifts from beneath the enormous tree, hair tousled and eyes warm and sleepy, was almost enough to make him say yes.

Only the barest grasp of sanity intervened. Cash and Mallory might be selling the place.

Which meant he'd better find a new home.

"Can't," he said. "My leave is up."

And when an older man he recognized from a

neighboring ranch came looking for her, Maverick slipped away through the crowd, keeping one careful eye out for that mistletoe.

You couldn't be too careful when it came to Mallory.

CHAPTER 2

"Maverick! Hey, Mav!"

Surrounded by a bevy of high school cheerleaders and his football team, Sam accepted high fives and hugs all around.

The football stadium was emptying out around them. They'd won. Again.

And everyone thought it was because of him.

Somewhere between junior and senior year, Cash's popularity had rubbed off on Sam. Some girls had decided he looked just like the hero from some eighties movie and had given him the nickname Maverick, and it seemed to have stuck.

Or maybe his newfound popularity was because the football arm. He'd been recruited for quarterback, though he'd tried out for football only to get out of his house before and after school.

He didn't care about being popular. But having friends other than Cash meant he could still go out on nights when Cash was busy. Which meant staying away from his old man, who'd only gotten meaner as Sam had finally gotten big enough to fight back against his drunken fists.

Most of the time. His ribs twinged beneath the pads and jersey, reminding him of the lucky hit dad had gotten in last night.

"Sam!" Another voice called out, this one from outside of the ring of groupies surrounding him.

Sam looked over their heads to see Mallory standing on the second-to-the-bottom bleacher, waving him over.

One of the cheerleaders followed his gaze and then looked back to Sam with a smirk on her lips. "Somebody's got a crush, huh?"

He doubted it. Mallory was too smart to have a crush on a dunce like him.

But he'd seen the cheerleader target and ostracize one of their classmates on a whim. There was no way he wanted Mallory's high school career ruined before she even got to high school. Eighth grade girls were impressionable. At least that's what he'd overheard Mrs. Trudeau saying to her husband once.

"Doubt it," he said casually. He shrugged as if

Mallory were a nuisance and nothing more. "She's just Cash's kid sister. She follows him around like a puppy." Hopefully the reminder that Mallory was related to Cash, who'd been a part of the in-crowd much longer than Sam had, would be enough to keep the cheerleader from focusing on her.

The cheerleader narrowed her eyes. Crap. His distraction hadn't worked.

He shouldn't care. He was leaving for basic training right after graduation. He'd leave Sawyer Creek behind. Mallory Trudeau's high school worries wouldn't be his concern.

Plus, Mallory was too perceptive for her own good. Last time good old Dad had gotten in a lucky hit, she'd seen the bruise on his jaw and figured it out.

He could fool his "friends" and the hangers-on, but Mallory was different.

Which meant he couldn't be around her tonight.

He made himself smile down at the cheerleader. "You want to grab a hamburger with me?"

She lit up. "Of course!" She turned to her friend. "Maverick and I are getting some food. Wanna come?"

Maverick. Not Sam.

Maverick would leave Mallory behind. For her own good.

Escaping Mallory was more difficult than evading a sniper's sharp eye in a war zone.

Every time Maverick turned around, she was there. Dancing and laughing with a guy he knew from high school. Addressing one of the waiters, looking as if she were giving instructions. Smiling at him, even during a conversation with a middle-aged woman.

Kiss me hello.

What on earth had made her say something like that? He'd never given any hint that he might be attracted to her.

Even though he'd always found her irresistibly beautiful. He'd noticed it first on his eighteenth birthday, when she'd been only fourteen. He and Cash had been in the kitchen, snitching cookies like little kids. Mallory had come in fresh off a horse's back, her hair windswept and curling around her face, her cheeks flushed, and laughter sparkling in her blue eyes. At that moment, he'd experienced a visceral pull toward her.

A pull like he'd never known.

Even then, he'd understood that wanting Mallory was wrong. She was Cash's baby sister. Not for him.

She'd end up with someone like Howie. Someone with roots here. Someone who would stick around, not somebody who was gonna get shipped around the globe because of his job. She'd end up with someone who would be there for big events, like birthdays and anniversaries. The birth of a child.

He couldn't guarantee he'd be around for any of that.

But neither could he turn off his awareness of her. Right now, she was talking with a man about his pop's age, if his dad had lived. Arguing, really. The festive atmosphere had changed somewhat as the party had worn on and folks had imbibed on the flowing alcohol.

His protective instincts fired as he watched the guy lean into her personal space. Mav's feet started moving, his knee twinging, before he'd realized he was going to intervene.

Some of the other partygoers were starting to turn and watch as the guy's voice raised above the polite chatter.

"—been making promises for years, and it's not solved—"

Mallory's back was to Maverick, and he couldn't hear her answer, but her stance remained loose, unconcerned. As if this guy wasn't a threat, even though he was two times her size and getting in her face. Was she nuts?

Maverick elbowed his way between two older women who seemed content to stare at what was going down, now close enough to hear Mallory's soft-spoken response.

She was totally unruffled, no sense whatsoever of the danger she was in.

"...we've brought in the assayer, and—"

She didn't see it coming, but Maverick did. And he was close enough to do something about it.

"That's what you said six months ago!" The jerk lost his temper and threw one of his arms in what might've been a punch.

Except Maverick stepped between them, and the blow bounced ineffectually off his shoulder. It felt like a errant fly.

"You should back up," he said. His voice was pretty even considering he was a millisecond from decking the guy.

Mr. Fancy Suit was in Maverick's face now, his own face flushing red.

"Mav." Mallory put a hand on his forearm. "Everything's fine."

"It will be, once this guy steps back a little." He didn't blink.

Dude finally got the message that Maverick wasn't joking and moved back a half-step. His Adam's apple bobbed.

"Maverick, this is our neighbor, Jim Keller. He owns the ranch to the west."

He didn't care who the heck this guy was. He didn't want anyone threatening Mallory.

But she moved around him as smoothly as if he were a rock in the river and she the flowing water.

"Jim, Cash or I will get back with you later this week. We will get this issue resolved."

She extended her hand and the other guy shook it. He sent Maverick a hooded glance over her shoulder as he walked away.

Mallory whirled on him. But instead of the grateful smile Maverick expected, she got right up in his grill.

"You are an overprotective ox!" Her words were delivered with the biggest, fakest smile he'd ever seen. She patted his chest, over his lapel, then gave him a little shove. He backed into one of the hallways that branched off the ballroom. It was dim, and the voices from the party were muted.

"I had everything under control," she said.

"That's not what it looked like." He didn't recognize the protective urge that had risen up in him when that yahoo had gotten in her face. He'd wanted to punch first and ask questions later.

She shook her head. "I'm not sure what Cash told you, but I'm a grown woman. I help run this ranch."

She was too oblivious. He stepped closer so he could keep his voice down. He wanted to scoop her up and carry her off somewhere safe until his heart rate came down.

"That guy had a hundred pounds on you. He could've knocked you down, knocked you out with one blow."

MAVERICK'S big body closed in, and Mallory took an instinctive step back, which put her shoulder blades against the wall. Her irritation fled in a rush of warmth as she recognized the emotion in his eyes.

He was worried for her.

Which meant that he cared.

She could work with that.

She let one hand rest against his chest. And he didn't move out of her space.

"I've had to grow up a lot this past year," she said softly. "Cash, too."

She watched his eyes darken. He'd loved her parents, too. Cash had told her Maverick wouldn't be able to get leave for the funeral, and he'd been right. She'd been lost in her own grief, but she'd wondered who would comfort him when he was so far away. Had anyone?

Now was not the time to ask.

"If I can inoculate a herd of five hundred bovines, I can handle one neighbor irate over a fencing dispute."

Maverick's eyes narrowed. His wide hands came to span her waist, heating her up from the inside out. "If he'd hit you—"

She laughed a little. "There's no way he was going to do something like that in the middle of a big crowd, most of whom are his friends and neighbors."

He squeezed her slightly. "What about the next time you're out checking the fence line.

What if he's armed when he wants to *talk* to you?"

"What if he's not?" She let her hand slide up to his shoulder. His rapid-fire breaths had finally evened out. "This dispute has been going on for over a year, ever since he bought the place next door. There are attorneys involved, and frankly, he's in the wrong. It'll get resolved, and he'll start acting neighborly."

It wasn't as big of a deal as Maverick thought it was. She and Cash had been dealing with it since they'd been appointed joint executors of their parents' estate. Jim might bluster, but he wasn't going to *hurt* her.

Maverick shook his head, the expression on his face one she remembered from their growing up years. He usually wore it when he couldn't believe something stupid she or Cash was doing. But this time, she was right.

Then, Maverick shifted, a slight wince crinkling the corners of his eyes.

She looked down, eyeing his left leg. He seemed to be favoring it, though it was very slight.

"Are you hurt?" she asked. Cash hadn't mentioned an injury, but that didn't mean anything. Sometimes her brother and Maverick had a code of silence that not even she could break.

"Nothing big."

Nothing big. His knee, maybe? The same one he'd hurt in a high school football game senior year?

She stared up into his face, waiting for him to explain.

But judging by the stubborn set of his jaw, he wasn't going to tell her.

She stifled her disappointment. The night was young.

She suddenly realized exactly where they were. A semi-private hall. With mistletoe hung strategically from the ceiling, a couple of yards away. It wasn't directly overhead, but she shouldn't waste this opportunity.

"We managed to find a bit of privacy," she whispered. "And that." She tipped her head toward the mistletoe ball hanging from the ceiling by a red ribbon.

Maverick followed her gaze, and she saw recognition register on his face. He glanced back down at her, at her lips, her eyes, and she saw it for a split second that he wanted to kiss her.

She let her eyes fall closed, tipped her mouth up—

But instead of pulling her closer, his hands flexed on her hips and then released her completely.

Her eyes flew open. She wobbled on the ridiculous heels as he pulled away, letting a rush of cooler air fill the space between their bodies.

All the warmth in his expression had disappeared. "Mallory..." He exhaled roughly, shoving a hand through his hair. "I can't. We can't."

She stepped toward him. "Can't what? Can't express our affection for each other?"

A quick burst of what might be panic flared in his eyes as she advanced on him. He took a step toward the ballroom.

"We've been friends a long time," he said. "*Friends.*"

She shrugged. "Friends can kiss, can't they?"

But she meant more than a simple brush of the lips, and he knew it. At least she thought he did.

"No."

She laughed. "Of course they can."

She reached out with both hands, and he captured them in his. He just held her there, almost two arms-length away. Not threading their fingers together. Just keeping her in place.

"Mallory." The seriousness in his voice stopped her advance. His face held traces of some emotion she couldn't define. "Mal, there's no mistletoe magic for us tonight. Or ever."

Oh. He didn't want to kiss her. She'd read him all wrong.

Someone called out to him, and he let her hands go, looking over his shoulder.

She hadn't realized just how far she'd chased him across the hallway. *She'd* chased *him*.

Maybe she'd imagined the quick glance to her lips.

Maybe she'd been letting her imagination run away with her for years.

Heat flared in her face, probably streaking red through her cheeks. She was not an attractive blusher.

Maverick looked back at her. His face was filled with concern. Worry that he'd hurt her feelings. Nothing more.

She shored up her smile. "I think that was Aaron Nichols." One of his friends from high school. "You'd better go say hi."

He was only in town for the night, after all.

His gaze held until she felt so brittle she feared her smile might crack. *I'm fine,* she telegraphed to him.

She'd come back from the depths of her grief after last Christmas.

She'd bounce back from this rejection.

Eventually.

CHAPTER 3

Maverick hated that he'd stolen Mallory's Christmas magic, broken her smile.

It was shocking to him that no one else had noticed. The ballroom seemed to have swelled with even more ranchers, cowboys, wives, and girlfriends, even though the snow was coming down harder, swirling in the dark outside the windows, visible thanks to the twinkle lights that wound around the arbor leading to the kitchen vegetable garden.

He'd taken up a stationary position near the hors d'oeurves table, ready to retreat if she came on the advance again.

He'd barely been able to refuse her once. He'd nearly had her in his arms. As it was he couldn't get the feel of her out of his head, her waist soft and slender between his hands, her lashes fluttering closed as she waited for his kiss.

He was an idiot.

He'd *had* to refuse her.

But the look in her eyes, the one she'd quickly banked... It had hit him like a mortar blast to his most vulnerable parts.

He hated hurting her feelings, but there was no future for them. It was better this way.

He'd gotten caught up in a conversation with a high school buddy who wanted to reminisce about their glory days as senior football players. Most of Maverick's memories from those days weren't the same as the those of the kids he'd graduated with.

If he rubbed the golden finish on them too hard, it was sure to tarnish. Good old Dad had made sure of that.

But he smiled and made small talk anyway, pretending things had been fine, the same way he'd pretended back then.

Cash was the only one who knew.

"Have you seen Mallory?" Speaking of his best friend.

Maverick turned to see Cash, who looked rumpled and annoyed. His hair was out of place, as if he—or someone else—had run his hands through it. And his tie was askew.

"Problem?" Maybe one of the party guests had had too much champagne and gotten rough?

Cash rubbed the back of his neck, looking both sheepish and annoyed at the same time. "Just... a staffing thing. Sort of. For the party."

A staffing thing. A thing.

A woman thing?

Maverick glanced across the room to see Mallory slip into the hallway that would lead back to the kitchen, formal dining room, and mud room. *Please don't let her be heading back there to cry.* If she'd told Cash that Maverick had had his hands on her, would he flatten him?

"She probably wants to enjoy the party like everyone else," Maverick suggested. "Can't a staffing problem wait until tomorrow?"

Cash's eyes flashed with annoyance. "No." He sighed. "You're right, though. Mallory has worked late nights for weeks to get this party to go off without a hitch. I'll deal with it."

He clapped a hand on Maverick's shoulder and walked off, apparently looking for his *staffing problem.*

Mallory didn't re-appear. Maverick let one

minute tick by, then two. She still hadn't returned.

He shouldn't go after her. Definitely not.

But his feet carried him around the perimeter of the ballroom anyway until he was ducking down that same hall.

The formal dining room was dark and empty of partygoers, and he quickly passed by the long, elegant table—perfect for a big, bustling family— and into the kitchen, where bright overhead lights shone. This room was filled with workers rushing around.

Crossing the threshold caused a pang of grief he hadn't expected. The kitchen was where Mrs. Trudeau had *lived.* If he squinted, he could imagine her there, standing at the sink, chiding him to wash his hands and come help with the supper preparations.

He breathed through the unexpected pain.

Mallory wasn't there either. A woman in a chef's coat and hat was directing servers who carried plates of tiny, fancy food. She stopped mid-sentence when she caught sight of him.

"Catering staff only," chef-lady said.

"Did Mallory Trudeau come in here?"

She looked him up and down, must've seen

how serious he was. She jerked her thumb toward the mudroom.

So. Mallory had been so upset that she was hiding out. This was all his fault. He had to fix it. Somehow.

Without kissing her.

He ducked through the doorway and found her at the back door, shrugging into a coat, one long enough that it swallowed her up from shoulders to calves. Right over her fancy party dress. She looked like a little kid playing dress up. He blinked, and it was a woman who looked back at him with soft eyes.

His stomach lurched.

Cash was gonna kill him if he didn't un-screw this up.

"Mal," he started. He didn't see any tears running down her face, but so what? He hadn't exactly been gentle with her earlier.

"Everything okay?" she asked. And then she bent over, slipping one stockinged foot into a barn work boot. Her glittery, strappy heels were on the floor beside her.

"That's what I followed you in here to ask. Did I... I didn't mean to hurt your feelings earlier. Come back to the party."

She glanced his way as she pulled on the second boot. Her scrunched brows showed her puzzlement, but her expression cleared as she straightened. Her lips twitched slightly.

"My feeling that we should take advantage of that mistletoe right above your head hasn't changed."

He looked up. Nothing there.

"Gotcha." When he looked back at her, she was grinning.

He mock-scowled. "Mal. I'm trying to get out a serious apology here."

She shrugged. "No apology needed."

"Then why are you running away? That sure seems like you're taking the hurt feelings thing to a pretty high level."

Now she laughed. He'd always loved the sound of her laugh, but he hated being the object of it.

He didn't think anything about this was funny. And he wanted to get back to the party before Cash started looking for his sister again.

"You've sure got a high opinion about your-self," she said.

Now his scowl turned real. But she wasn't done.

"Here." She grabbed an iPad off the counter that ran along the back wall and tossed it his way.

He caught it reflexively, thankful that it had one of those reinforced cases on it. Ranch life was rough.

She was pulling on gloves.

"Mal," he started again. What the heck was she doing?

"Look," she insisted.

He glanced down at the screen. It was a black and white photo—no, there was slight movement. It was a video. A horse was lying down in a big box stall. Was that—? It seemed to be the birthing stall. He'd known every inch of the barn, explored it inside and out.

"Is she foaling?" he asked.

"It's a gelding. Prince. He'd been acting funny, off his feed this morning. If he's down, I'm worried it's colic."

Prince. Her dad's horse.

Every cowboy worth his salt knew that colic could be deadly if untreated. But she was in a party dress—

And now looping a scarf around her neck. Reaching for the door. Was she crazy?

"Mal—"

"I gotta go."

She pulled the door open, and in swirled snow and a wind that chilled him from head to toe.

There was no way he was letting her go out to the barn in a blizzard. That dress was no protection at all, even with a coat on. What if her truck got stranded on the half-mile trip?

She glanced over her shoulder, halfway out the door. "If I don't see you again tonight, stay safe."

"Mallory."

She ignored him, letting the door snap shut behind her.

He growled a curse word under his breath and went to the pegs where Cash's work coat hung. He shrugged it on, a tight fit even though his friend was muscled from working the ranch.

And he went out into the cold after her.

"YOU ARE NOT DRESSED for this, woman."

Mallory registered the big body behind her only because he blocked the wind from her back as she wrenched open the door to the farm truck.

Maverick had followed her outside.

She was turning to tell him off—she did *not* need a big brother riding drag, and apparently he never planned on being anything but a big brother.

"Get *in*," he said, and his hands were at her lower back, boosting her into the truck. And then urging her across the bench seat as he followed.

He pulled the door shut, and the silence in the cab was absolute. Except it wasn't. She could hear the howling wind outside, hear both of them breathing ragged breaths, hear the thud of her heart in her ears.

There was no ignoring the sheer presence of the man.

He blew on his cupped hands, then glanced her way. "Keys."

It wasn't a question, and his presumption made her want to refuse. He was just like a bossy older brother.

Except he wasn't her brother. Not even close.

And it was freezing in the truck. She handed

them over. They plunked into the palm of his hand with the force behind her movement.

"I don't need you to drive me to the barn."

"You should've sent Cash to the barn," he snapped. He cranked the ignition, and the truck turned over.

His left hand lowered absently to massage his knee. Did he even realize he'd done it?

Did the cold bother his injury? How bad was it? She bit back the questions, knowing he wouldn't appreciate her asking, not after he'd shut her down at the party.

"Prince is my horse now." Prince had been Dad's faithful horse. He deserved the best care, and she intended to deliver it. Her entire night of frustration over the man beside her made her words tart. "I can take care of the problem myself. I don't need your help."

He mumbled something under his breath and looked at her with squinted eyes. "You ever driven in a whiteout?"

She stared him down. "Have you?"

His eyes narrowed even more. "No. I can't remember if we've ever had one in this part of Texas."

Ha.

"But I've piloted a Humvee through a sand storm."

She gritted her teeth. She didn't need a big brother. And humiliation was still a hot stone in her chest. There was no way she was getting rid of him. So they should just get it over with.

She gestured toward the road, eyebrows raised.

He put the truck in gear and let off the brake, allowing them to roll forward. The snow was so thick, it was impossible to see anything beyond the flakes flying in the headlights.

"You'd better hope your brother sends the party home, or you'll have a houseful of guests staying the night."

She'd seen the forecast. It wasn't supposed to stick.

Of course, the weatherman hadn't predicted a whiteout blizzard like this either.

"Visibility is too low," she said. She popped open the glove compartment to grab the flashlight inside. Flicked it on. Batteries were strong. "Stop for a second and let me out. I'll walk ahead and make sure you keep to the road."

He grabbed her arm before she'd even

reached for the door handle. "Not in that getup, you won't."

"It's not like there was time to go change. If I'd have tried going back through the ballroom, I'd have been grabbed six or seven times with people wanting to talk to me." And the spare pair of jeans she'd left in the mudroom had been muddied last week, and she'd forgotten to replace them.

"Besides, the barn is heated."

"If we make it to the barn," he mumbled.

"My horse's life might be in danger," she said. "We have to make it. I'll lean out the window. You remember the way to the barn?"

He shot her a look that she couldn't help returning with a grin. He'd been as horse-crazy as she and Cash during their growing up years.

She rolled down the window, ratcheted up the heater, then levered her knees up on the seat and leaned out the window. Maverick let the truck roll forward in the blinding snow, barely nudging the gas pedal. The snow had already accumulated maybe an inch, but it would pile up quickly at this rate.

Maybe Maverick would get snowed in. If

enough snow accumulated that he couldn't dig out....

That was wishful thinking. He'd been pretty adamant about not kissing her. She'd joked about it in the mudroom, because she didn't want him to feel sorry for her.

He didn't want her, after all.

It wasn't like she had a ton of experience with men. One short-term boyfriend in high school and a couple of failed relationships in college.

Maverick traveled the world. No doubt he was used to worldly women. Could talk about subjects that you might see in the national news. He had no interest in a small-town girl who knew more about cattle and hay prices than geopolitics.

She'd been so sure...

Now she didn't feel sure of anything.

Besides, Prince was in danger. She aimed the flashlight to the ground, to the inch of snow obscuring the grass and gravel on the barn lane. There wasn't so much accumulation that she wouldn't be able to tell if they veered off the road.

"You're fine," she told Maverick over her shoulder. "Hit the gas."

She heard the sound of his grunt over the roar of the wind in her ears.

Then his big, warm hand closed over her calf where her party dress had ridden up and left only her stocking exposed above the boot.

He held onto her leg loosely. Maybe he was afraid she'd lean too far and fall headfirst out of the truck.

But since her head was stuck in the blinding snow and he couldn't see the emotion on her face, she pretended he'd put his hand there because he wanted to hold her.

CHAPTER 4

MAVERICK ALMOST PLOWED INTO THE BARN. Luckily, he was only going five miles per hour, so when the side of the barn appeared out of the near-blinding snow, he jammed on the brakes and stopped the truck before they wrecked.

Barely.

Mallory didn't react to his abrupt stop, just pulled herself back into the cab and reached for the button that would roll up the window.

Her head was covered in snow. She was trying not to give away that she was shivering.

He let out a strangled, "Mal—" and hauled her over the middle seat and into his arms. With the window closed now, the heater was blasting hot air that would soon be stifling in the small enclosed space.

Mallory clung to his chest, still trying to hide her trembling. It hadn't been that long, maybe ten minutes to traverse the road to the barn. Not long enough for her to be in danger.

But he didn't push her away.

He brushed melting snow out of her hair. It clung to her eyelashes, clumping them together.

He cupped her jaw, the pad of his thumb catching a melted snowflake before it dripped down her cheek.

He'd obviously killed his sense of self-preservation somewhere during the two overseas deployments.

Because she was even closer now than she'd been earlier.

And he really wanted to kiss her.

He couldn't, even though holding her this close made all the reasons why fuzzy and hard to remember. Cash.

He bent his head...

And at the last moment, moved to press his cheek to hers. Her skin was chilled and moist, her hair curling in damp ringlets that he desperately wanted to bury his nose in.

"This was a horrible idea," he muttered.

She pushed on his chest, and he let her go.

Hopefully she was warm enough, because he was burning up. She scooted across the seat with a huff. "I'm not going to let Prince die because it's snowing."

She opened her door, and the wind was blowing so hard that it almost closed back on her. With a grunt, she shoved it again and then slipped out into the howling wind.

He turned off the truck and followed her into the blizzard. It was only feet to the barn door, but he felt battered by the time they both got inside.

At least it was warm, the heaters working merrily.

He fell a step behind Mallory's march toward the birthing stall at the back of the barn.

The scent of hay and horses—even the manure—brought him back viscerally to those fleeting moments in his childhood and teenage years when Cash had dragged him out here. Learning about horses and doing chores.

For those few hours, he'd pretended he was a part of their family. A real part, not just a kid from town that the Trudeaus felt sorry for.

He'd wanted to stay forever.

He hadn't been allowed, because he hadn't

belonged. No amount of wishing or dreaming would change that.

And it wouldn't change anything now.

Cash belonged.

Mallory belonged. Even though she didn't look it right now, with her mismatched outfit—the evening gown with her barn boots and the work coat.

He couldn't help a shake of his head and a smile. Mallory'd always marched to her own beat. It was something he admired about her.

Even he could tell the horse was in distress when they reached the stall. Mallory had ducked into the tack room and now held a small duffel bag.

He followed her into the stall. Knelt at Prince's head as she made quick work of looking in his mouth, taking his temperature, and then checking his heart rate. Rote, like she'd performed the routine dozens of times.

He rubbed Prince's nose. "Hello, old mate."

How many hours had he spent on the back of a horse, chasing Cash across the fields, scaring quail out of the long summer grasses, and wishing? Mr. Trudeau had been present in many of those memories, riding right alongside them. A good dad.

Emotion choked his throat, surprising him.

He brushed his hand across nose and stood. "What do we need to do?"

She looked up at him from where she knelt at the horse's flank. He could see the surprise in her eyes. Because he'd allied himself?

It wasn't for forever. Only for tonight, the few hours he had left.

He'd help her save the horse, because he couldn't do anything else.

"We need to get him up." She stood too, stowing the thermometer in her bag and then hanging the bag over the railing. She unhooked a lead rope and attached it to the horse's halter.

"Should we call the vet?" he asked. Would a veterinarian be able to get out here in a snowstorm like this?

"I had enough schooling before mom and dad died to administer a stomach tube, if we need it. Sometimes just getting a horse up and moving is enough to release some of the tension in his gut."

He'd known she'd had to put school on hold when her parents died. He'd forgotten—let himself forget maybe—how passionate she'd been about being a vet.

He moved to the horse's rear and gave a gentle slap as Mallory coaxed the horse from its head.

"You're going back, right?" he asked.

He hated to think about her giving up on her dreams because of the accident.

She urged the horse with soft words. Then to Maverick, "No, I'm not going back."

"Why not? Once you and Cash sell the ranch, you'll have your life back."

She looked up at him, brow furrowed. "We aren't selling the ranch."

THE UTTER SHOCK on Maverick's face would've been comical if the subject had been less serious.

She jerked her focus to the horse. Prince pawed his front feet against the ground.

"C'mon, boy. You got this."

Maverick shifted out of the way as the horse pushed to his feet.

Mallory ached at the tentative way he rose, knowing he was in pain.

"Good boy." She didn't stop to pat his neck,

knowing that keeping him moving was the most important thing. She had to believe that Prince was going to be okay.

She didn't look back as she guided Prince by the lead in a slow meander out of the stall and down the length of the barn. She didn't have to look to know that Maverick hung back.

Her statement had thrown him. Why had he thought she and Cash would give up their family legacy?

He stood in the open stall door when she and Prince walked back, arms crossed and with one shoulder propped against the wall. It was a casual pose, But she knew better. She could read the line of tension in his spine.

"Mom and Dad would've been glad to see you back where you belong," she said.

Maybe it was the wrong thing to say, because his tension seemed to ratchet up a notch. She'd wanted to get him to open up, share some of the grief he must be feeling on his first time back to the Double Cross.

But he only frowned.

So she tried a different track. "Where did you hear that I was selling?"

He didn't move, his stillness betraying more

than he probably wanted. "Something Cash said. That y'all were thinking about a change."

She turned the horse around, passing close enough to get a whiff of Maverick's spicy cologne. "We are."

A muscle jumped in his jaw but then she was past him. She didn't want to shout over her shoulder, Prince was anxious enough as it was with the stomach pain.

Plus, Maverick was too emotional about this subject. Let him stew a while longer.

Something was going on. She might be relegated to the friend-zone, but that didn't mean she stopped caring about him. Something was eating at him.

He was the one who called out to her on her way back, though he kept his voice even and calm. "So what does that mean then, that you're making a change?"

"I'm hiring a foreman and Cash is going back to work in Austin."

"He's leaving *you* to run the Double Cross?"

The skepticism in his voice had her chin jerking toward the roof. "You don't think I can handle it? I didn't realize you were such a chauvinistic pig."

Back ramrod straight, she marched away, only at the last second realizing that she might endanger the horse if she didn't calm down.

Who cared what Maverick thought, anyway? He wasn't sticking around. He was leaving before the sun came up.

She'd run this ranch as good as Daddy ever did. She'd prove Maverick wrong. Even if he weren't here to see it.

Prince pulled back on the lead, neighing. She let her eyes roam the horse and concluded that he must be reading her tension. She worked to release the tension in her shoulders, loosen her fingers on the lead rope.

As they walked toward the opposite end of the barn, she started recounting all seven hundred muscles in the horse's anatomy.

She'd just pretend Maverick had stayed up at the house. Or send him back. That was the answer.

When she returned to his end of the barn, Maverick still hadn't moved. His eyes followed her every step.

She forced a smile she didn't feel. "Why don't you head back up to the house? You probably want to spend some time with Cash before you leave town. Now that Prince is up, I'll be fine out here."

Maverick's eyes narrowed. "I'm not leaving you alone in the barn in a blizzard."

"Stop being so overprotective. I'm not some fainting miss from a romance novel or something."

"How're you going to get home, if I take the truck?"

She shrugged. "I'll take one of the four-wheelers." They used them often in the warmer months to check on the herds. "Or I'll call Cash on the barn phone," she added when Maverick's frown tightened. "I'm a big girl. I can figure it out."

He opened his mouth to say something, but then must've thought better of it, because his mouth snapped shut.

"I'm here for the duration," he snapped.

She sighed. "It might be hours before this horse poops, Mav. You don't owe me anything. My feelings aren't hurt. Just go."

She turned away, walking the horse toward the other end of the barn. And she didn't look back, because she didn't want to watch him go.

And she surely didn't want him to see the lie in her eyes.

This night was a disaster. Nothing had gone the way she'd hoped.

She'd wanted a kiss. More, she'd wanted Maverick to open up to her.

Maverick, who apparently still thought of her as an annoying ten-year-old little sister.

Hot tears rose behind her eyes. She blinked rapidly, refusing to let the stupid cowboy-slash-soldier see that he'd upset her.

This time, when she turned back, he was gone.

CHAPTER 5

A FOURTEEN-YEAR-OLD *SAM AND* CASH *LOUNGED ON
the couch in the Trudeau's living room, watching a
zombie movie with the lights down low. Crumbs were
the only evidence of the plate of brownies Mrs.
Trudeau had sent in here with them.*

Suddenly, the lights flipped on.

*A wild war whoop preceded Mallory into the
room, but not by much. She launched herself in a
cannonball into the center couch cushion. Sam got
kicked in the stomach and let out an "oof!"*

"Ma-al!" Cash wailed. Then shouted. "Mom!"

*Mallory ignored her brother, swiping the TV
remote from the coffee table. "Mom said it was my
turn to watch whatever I want." She sent a sly wink in
Sam's direction before she flipped the channel.
Another movie came on, this one with two dogs and a*

cat. Talking animals traversing... the Rocky Mountains?

There was a reason Cash called his sister Mal-Monster.

"She did not!" Cash reached for the remote, but Mallory held it out of his reach.

"You love this movie," Mallory teased. "Tell Sam how it's your favorite movie ever."

Cash growled and pounced on his sister, going for her sides with tickling claws.

Mallory shrieked and wriggled, but Cash had her pinned to the couch. "Sam, help!"

She got in a knee to his gut, and Cash grunted. "No way. Sam's on my side. C'mon, man. Hold her arms!"

Mallory's head bumped his shoulder, and Sam scooted until he was pressed against the arm of the couch.

The wrestling match continued. In six years of being absorbed into the Trudeau family as Cash's best friend, he'd seen plenty of wrestling matches. Cash didn't always win. Mallory knew just where to pinch her brother to get him to back off—and when to call in Mom for support.

Sam had never joined in. He was a little afraid of being too rough and accidentally hurting Mallory. She *was so much smaller—and a girl. And if he did anything that made the Trudeaus mad at him, he might get invited to leave. And not come back.*

"Mo-om!" Cash hollered. "Mallory's interrupting me and Cash!"

Maybe Mrs. Trudeau had gone outside, because she didn't come see what was going on.

Mallory got in another lucky knee and Cash howled. "Ooww!"

"Ha ha!" Mallory crowed.

Sam kind of liked it when she whipped up on her big brother.

And when he felt her slip the remote between his back and the couch cushions, he didn't let on.

Before the Trudeaus, he'd never seen movies with princesses and fairy tales. They weren't all awful, no matter how much Cash complained.

Besides, zombies made his stomach ball up like when Dad had his first beer of the night.

He didn't figure it was cool to say so, though, now that he and Cash were high school freshmen.

So he'd just let Mallory say it for him, for now.

MAVERICK PACED the tiny office in the back of the barn. The room couldn't be more than ten by ten and apparently the heating vent was right over-head, because it was sweltering in here.

A heavy wooden desk that he remembered from years ago was spread with papers. Some-body'd put a small potted fir tree on the edge of the desk closest to the wall, and although it didn't have lights, it was covered in silk balls and hand-cut snowflakes.

Other than the tree, there were tallies, sale invoices, and who knew what spread across the desk. And almost all of them were covered with *Mallory's* handwriting.

Because she was taking over the ranch.

He'd never in a million years thought that Cash's statement about making a change meant that he'd be abandoning Mallory.

What about her dreams?

Maverick knew her well enough to know that if he'd kept arguing with her, she'd have dug in her heels. If she'd made up her mind, he would be hard-pressed to change it.

But he was used to impossible challenges.

And he couldn't bear for his friend to throw away her whole life.

He just needed a way to show her the truth.

He eyeballed the chipped, faded and stained

cabinet hung above the desk in the back corner. Cash's dad had always kept a couple of cans of beans up there. Who knew why? In case he got stuck out here and had to survive? When he and Cash had been teenagers, the labels had already been faded.

Any chance they were still there?

They weren't. Inside the cabinet were a box of granola bars, a can of hot chocolate mix, and several bottles of water.

Mallory really had taken over.

But maybe this would give him a way to start a conversation.

He found two mugs behind the box of granola bars and wiped them out with a paper towel before he poured some of the bottled water in them and then nuked them in the microwave on the back desk.

He mixed up the cocoa and while a memory stirred in his subconscious.

He must've been thirteen, which would've put Mallory at nine. They'd been caught on the ranch in a thunderstorm with the power out, and Cash's mom had made them hot chocolate over a camp stove. They'd sat around the kitchen table by candlelight, drinking until they had chocolate mustaches.

And when Cash's mom left the room, Mallory had been quick to scamper to a lower cabinet. She'd returned to the table with a bag of mini marshmallows.

"Can't have hot chocolate without these," she'd whispered conspiratorially. She'd dropped ten of the things into his cup, and they'd quickly expanded, covering the liquid from edge to edge and making it impossible to drink.

He'd given it a shot, anyway, because she and Cash were the only people who shared anything with a kid from the wrong side of town.

Mallory's gap-toothed grin had been worth it.

He squinted a little, crossing behind the desk and scouring for...

He opened the desk drawer and grabbed out the half-eaten pack of marshmallows that had been rolled up and tucked in a zipper bag.

It was a wonder she didn't have mice everywhere. She must have a good barn cat, though he hadn't caught sight of one.

Before he could pull the bag from its hiding place, his knuckle brushed against something cool and smooth, something out of sight beneath a sheaf of papers.

Curiosity surged and he changed objectives and pulled a picture frame from the drawer.

He'd expected a photo of her parents or maybe a favorite horse, but it wasn't either of those.

It was a framed photo from his high school graduation. He and Cash had been in caps and gowns. So young. She'd run up behind him and jumped on his back like a monkey. He'd been flying high that day. Ready for the freedom that was due to him.

He'd laughed and given her a piggyback ride, and Cash's mom had caught the moment with the three of them together—him, Cash, and Mallory on his back. He'd been laughing. A moment of joy interrupting a string of awful childhood memories.

She'd kept this photo of him. A tiny part of his brain niggled that the photo was the three of them.

But he knew.

She'd kept it because of the photo of *him*.

Hot emotion, even more than what he'd felt when he'd seen Prince again, rose up in his chest.

He stifled it.

Nothing had changed.

She was anchored here, on the Double Cross. Determined to ruin her life.

His leave was almost up. He was career military.

And she was Cash's little sister. Cash, who knew just how flawed Maverick was. Who would never agree to let his little sister slum with him.

Maverick shoved down every little whisper inside that begged him to find a way to belong here.

He never had, and he never would.

MALLORY JUMPED when she caught sight of Maverick exiting the tiny hallway that led to both the tack room and her barn office.

He was carrying two mugs. Steam wafted from the tops.

"What're you still doing here?" She'd thought he had finally wised up and gone back to the house.

"I told you I'm not leaving you down here by yourself."

She drew Prince to a momentary stop, gave

the lead rope slack as she approached Maverick. "Is that for me?"

"Yeah." He handed her the mug. His eyes were hooded, unreadable.

She drew the mug up without looking at it and had to laugh when a massive float of marshmallows bumped her upper lip.

"You found my stash." She smiled up at him.

A corner of his mouth quirked, but he seemed to be too busy scouring her face—for what? —to smile.

"I remember how you liked it."

She laughed again. "Yeah, when I was ten." She took a sip anyway, though the sweetness from the marshmallows threatened to overpower the cocoa itself.

He took a sip from his mug and then put it on the nearest flat-topped post. He reached out one hand. "Let me have a turn."

She handed over the lead rope, not because she needed a break but because something had made the light in his eyes darken in the twenty minutes since he'd disappeared into her office.

Maybe it was impulsive, but before she let go of the lead rope, she rose on tiptoes and brushed a kiss across his stubbled cheek.

She turned her shoulder before he could remind her about her place in the friend zone.

She breathed easier when he started walking, Prince in tow, without commenting.

She couldn't help the way her gaze followed the man. He'd shrugged Cash's work coat off at some point and now looked completely out of place in his tuxedo, walking alongside the horse. She supposed she looked just as foolish in her evening gown and work boots.

She could hear him talking to the horse, but his words were too low to make out.

She forced her focus to Prince. His agitation had eased some as she'd walked him. He'd stopped pulling against the lead to try and roll. If the colic were worsening, he would've kept trying to lie down.

She was optimistic. Prince was Dad's horse. He'd been on the ranch since she was little. She'd ridden him with dad before she could walk. He'd done his working duty as a cutting horse and was now enjoying old age and the occasional amble through the property when she had time. He'd worked hard. He deserved it.

How many nights had Dad missed sleep over

an animal? Too many to count. In some small way, tonight made her feel closer to him.

She didn't want to see Prince in pain, and she only hoped this colic was a passing thing, an issue from something he'd eaten that would pass and never return.

Now it was a waiting game. *How long until the horse pooped?*

The cocoa was too sweet for her—not the childhood her, but she wasn't ten anymore, and it was about time Maverick noticed—and she traded it for his mug. He had two mini-marshmallows floating in his.

She considered the man as he walked beside the horse.

What had put the guarded look in Maverick's eyes?

She could ask but doubted he would answer. He'd never opened up to her the way he had with Cash. She was younger. And a girl.

That didn't mean she didn't know things. She'd been a master eavesdropper when she was a kid. She'd once climbed a neighboring tree when Cash and Maverick had been tucked into the tree fort they'd cobbled together in a gully not far from the house.

She'd listened for an hour as Cash raged against Maverick's dad, calling him curse words she'd never heard before. Maverick had said barely anything.

When she'd snuck back to the house, she'd asked her mom what one of the words meant and gotten an earful about the foul language she must have overheard at school.

When the boys had come in later, she'd seen the bruise darkening Maverick's right cheekbone.

He hadn't looked her in the eye that day.

How had he survived a childhood like that and turned into the honorable soldier he was now?

What would it be like to have Maverick's trust?

What would it take to earn it?

In an hour.

She shook her head a little, laughing at herself. She was so desperate for tonight not to end, for Maverick not to disappear again, that her thoughts continued to run away with her.

Better to distract herself.

She'd meant to decorate the barn for Christmas, but with the Cattlemen's Ball, she'd been too busy. Why not now, since she was stuck out here anyway waiting on a horse to poop?

She went to the tack room and found the giant box of decorations she'd put there last week. Then spent a good five minutes straining to push and pull it by turns along the floor to the main barn area.

When she finally stood from behind the box, she was huffing and puffing.

Maverick was approaching, and he couldn't hide the smile twitching across his lips. "Good job, Monster."

"Thanks"—she panted—"for your help."

He laughed. "What've you got in there? A robot to keep walking this guy?"

She shook her head. "Something better."

She took out the first faux-green wreath and held it up to show him.

His nose wrinkled comically. "Didn't you have enough decorations up at the house? It looked like Santa threw up in there."

She considered tossing the wreath at him. "Scrooge. You can never have enough decorations." She bent over the box, pretending to dig through it. "I might even have some fake mistletoe in here." Because she'd never put the real deal out here. It was toxic to animals.

He groaned. But it sounded like she might've jarred him out of whatever dark place he'd disappeared to a few moments ago.

She started hanging wreaths on each stall door, adjusting the velvet bows on each one and fluffing the fake greenery.

"What'd you get your brother for Christmas?" he asked as he passed behind her. He tugged on the ends of her hair but was past before she could swat him.

Apparently, they weren't going to talk about anything important tonight.

"New underwear and socks."

He snort-laughed. "You did not."

She glanced at him over her shoulder. "Did too. It's what Mom used to get him every year." Her throat clogged at the thought of Mom's precise wrapping and designer bows and how badly Mallory had botched that this year.

Oh, man.

And then Maverick was there, drawing her away from the stall door and her pile of decorations on the floor. And into his arms.

MAVERICK DIDN'T KNOW what had come over him.

Mallory clung to him, in that place between sniffling and all-out crying. Her face was pressed against his chest, and every breath she exhaled was hot through the linen of his shirt.

"Prince," she protested in a wet murmur, and he heard the unshed tears in her voice.

Maverick glanced behind him. "He's okay for now." The horse stood placidly in the middle of the aisle.

"I r-ruined the Thanksgiving turkey," she whispered, voice wobbling.

He pressed his nose into her hair, allowing the liberty he'd denied himself earlier. Holding Mallory was... everything. "How so?"

"I had the oven on too high. It came out burnt on the outside and raw inside."

He breathed out a chuckle. "Did you use a recipe?"

"No." She sniffled. "I thought I could remember the way Mom cooked it. But I was wrong."

His smile died. He cupped the back of her head with one hand, holding her close. She still didn't cry.

He pressed his jaw against her hair, brushed her ear. "You'll remember the important stuff. Like how your mom used to sing when she brushed your hair at night. I saw her do that once, when Cash invited me for a sleepover." Watching Mrs. Trudeau's soft touch had opened an ache inside him, one that would never be filled. He didn't have a mom.

Her arms around his back, she squeezed him. "You loved them, too."

He had. When he'd gotten Cash's voicemail from overseas, he'd been blown apart by grief.

It wasn't the same, he told himself. He wasn't their blood. But he had loved them.

She moved back slightly. Not out of his hold, but enough that there was a separation between their upper bodies.

"Is that what you do, when you're deployed? Remember the important stuff?" She said the words to his buttons.

Because she wasn't looking at him, he could look his fill. Memorize the dark sweep of her lashes against her cheeks. He really wanted to trace the soft line of her lips with his finger. He settled for smoothing her hair back from her face.

He'd never forget this moment.

Then she tipped her face up to look at him. Her eyes sparkled with unshed tears.

"Want to know what I got you for Christmas?"

She didn't wait for his answer but pressed up on tiptoe, her intention clear.

And because he was only human after all, he met her kiss. He tried to keep it light, gentle, because this was Mallory.

But this was *Mallory*.

"Maverick," she whispered against the brush of his lips.

She tilted her head, her lips slanting beneath his as he captured her mouth, plundered it.

As he got lost in her.

He tried to force himself to unlock his arms, loosen his grip on her, but she pressed even closer, and he was in so deep, too deep...

She was the one who pulled back, because he couldn't seem to her go. There'd been some slight noise that he hadn't registered. Until now.

Her eyes were soft and dreamy, her lips pink and beestung from his kisses.

She was sparkling up at him, shining from the inside. "I think…" She glanced over his shoulder, her mouth pursing slightly. "Yes, I think Prince has solved his problem."

She stepped fully out of his arms and at the loss, he felt cold.

And smelled manure.

"That's good, right?" Maverick half-turned away from her and ran one hand down his face, propping the other on his waist.

He was undone. Kissing Mallory had been perfect... So perfect that he'd forgotten himself completely.

And that was a problem.

She didn't seem to notice the sudden tension that gripped him, focused as she was on the horse.

"I want to take his vitals again," she said absently. "Do you want to check on the visibility? See if it's still snowing?"

"Sure." She didn't seem to hear him as she led the horse toward the big stall in the back.

A few minutes in the cold might do him good. Help him regain some equilibrium.

Outside, the wind had died out some, but snow fell in a deluge of huge, fluffy flakes. It was slightly less dangerous than earlier.

Is that what you do? Remember the important

stuff? He hadn't answered her question. But he did.

He thought about her all the time. Until he was sick over her, ached for her.

He'd never told anyone. And he wouldn't tell her tonight.

Coming here had been a mistake. Being on the Double Cross had opened old wounds, the grief he'd thought he'd battled and won. That's all this was. A mistake to kiss her, when his emotions were vulnerable and confused.

If he stayed in the barn with Mallory any longer, he was liable to make another mistake. Kiss her again.

Make promises they both knew he couldn't keep.

They needed to get back to the house, pronto.

CHAPTER 6

Prince's vitals looked stable, the color still good in his gums. Because he'd moved his bowels and had stopped trying to bite at his stomach, Mallory felt comfortable leaving him in the stall with the baby-monitor camera watching.

It was after midnight, and by all rights she should be exhausted. She'd been up at five a.m. to get all her ranch chores completed and prepare for the party.

She *was* tired, but she didn't want to miss a second with Maverick. She followed him to the truck and got in.

Relief and joy began to fade as she watched him.

He seemed distinctly uncomfortable as he sat behind the wheel, waiting for the defrost to warm up the windshield enough that they could see out of it.

He hadn't looked at her since that kiss. Kisses.

He'd been so passionate, had held her so closely. She'd hoped...

Well, she still wasn't some fainting miss.

"Do you regret kissing me?"

He finally glanced right at her, his expression slightly incredulous. Because she'd asked, or because he *did*?

His hands flexed on the wheel. He went back to staring out the white-covered windshield.

"No, I don't regret it."

Oh, thank goodness.

"But that doesn't mean we should do it again."

The joy bubbling up inside her like champagne bubbles popped. He didn't want a repeat. It was obvious he didn't want *her*. If he did, he'd have her sitting on the middle of the bench seat, not marooned over here. Tears caught in a knot in the back of her throat.

He slammed out of the truck, grabbing an ice scraper from the floorboards on his way. In minutes, he'd cleared the accumulated snow and ice from the windshield and gotten back in the truck.

He was covered in snow, but she felt colder than he looked.

She wrapped her arms around herself.

One quick glance at her, and he switched the heater from defrost to straight heat. It blew on her feet, but nothing was going to melt the ice inside of her.

She stared out her window. Realized he might be waiting on her.

"Do you need me to watch the road again?" she asked, watching his reflection in her window.

"No. Visibility is better."

He put the truck in reverse and carefully maneuvered a three-point turn so that the truck was pointed toward the house.

It was pitch dark out and the snow was still coming down. Visibility wasn't *that* much better. Obviously, he wanted to be rid of his troublesome problem. Cash's kid sister.

A minute passed in silence.

Then, "Tell me what happened with Howie."

Like she was going to respond to a demand like that? After he'd shut her down.

"Nothing happened," she said sweetly. To her window.

"You're lying."

She shrugged. "It's not your business."

She could practically hear him seething. "Does Cash know?"

"Not his business either." *Jingle bells*. She was a grown woman. She could handle her own problems.

He growled under his breath. "Just tell me what happened."

Arms still crossed over her middle, she turned toward him in the seat.

He glanced at her and back to the road. His hands gripped the wheel so hard she imagined his knuckles were white beneath the gloves. Something was off with him, something more than this conversation.

"You really want to know? I'll tell you. *If* you tell me about your knee injury."

He scowled. "You mean the knee I busted up playing high school football?"

"I mean the knee you busted up, what... three months ago?"

Color filled his cheeks. So she was right. Or close, at least.

He bared his teeth in what would never count for a smile. "Fine. I busted my ACL on a mission."

"How long ago?"

His hands fisted on the wheel. "Fifteen weeks. I had surgery to repair it, and my recovery is almost over. Like my leave. Satisfied?"

He slowed the truck, leaning forward to see through the crazy blowing snow.

"Not nearly. Why didn't you come home?"

He shot her a quick look, one that was almost a glare. "I scrapped my dad's tin can of a trailer the day after he died."

"I was talking about the Double Cross."

His lips opened in a real snarl this time. "The Double Cross isn't my home."

"Y—"

Before she could finish, the wheel spun in his hands.

He gave a wordless shout, and his right arm flew out to block her from hitting the dash as the truck spun out of control. The right front wheel slipped off the embankment and, too quickly, they slid into the ditch.

She braced, too late, as the crash seemed to happen in slow motion. Her shoulder banged against the door. She settled at an angle, the seat belt cutting into her shoulder.

Then the truck shut off, the motor still ticking.

Silence fell.

Maverick was such a screw-up.

Humiliation surged as he panted through the terror of what had just happened.

Mallory was silent beside him. He looked her over, head to toe. No obvious injuries.

But she was visibly shaken.

"Mal, I'm sorry—"

She turned to him, blinking. She breathed in. Exhaled. "Are you okay?" she asked.

"The truck..."

She shook her head, unbuckling her seat belt. "It's insured. Are *you* okay?"

His own seat belt was cutting into his waist. If he took it off, he'd slide down the tilted seat toward her.

She reached out. Touched his shoulder. His knee panged, but that wasn't anything new.

Minutes ago, he'd wanted as much distance between them as he could get.

But her touch, her concern...

The back of his nose burned because she was worried about him.

"I'm fine," he said roughly.

She jiggled her door handle. "Can you open your door? How far do you think we are from the house?"

"Too far for you to walk in that dress," he said.

She rubbed both hands over her face. Reached into one coat pocket. Then the other. "I must've left my cell in the barn."

"I've got mine." He dug in his pocket and pulled out his phone. The screen lit, and he dialed Cash's number from memory.

Cash didn't answer. It rang to voicemail.

He pulled the phone from his ear and dialed again.

He glanced at Mallory as it rang in his ear. "He's not answering."

"It's been hours. You don't still think the party is going...?"

He shrugged, jiggling the phone loose from his face. He steadied it with his shoulder. "It's your party. How late did you expect it to go?"

She frowned. "No one expected this massive snowfall."

Cash didn't answer a second time. This time

when the phone kicked over to voicemail, Maverick left one. "It's me. Mallory and I ran off the road on the way back from the barn. We could use a lift back to the house. Call me back." He hung up. "What about the caterer?"

"Her number is in my phone," Mallory said with a frown. "I can walk. It can't be more than a quarter mile."

"*If* we manage to stay on the road in this storm. And slogging through this snow will take longer than usual. You aren't even wearing pants."

She frowned. "So... what do we do?"

"Wait a bit. See if Cash wakes up and sees his voicemail."

Gravity was doing its best to push him down onto her, and his knee was taking the brunt of his weight as he worked to keep from sliding on top of her.

"Why don't you just slide down here and quit hurting your knee," she said, her brow creasing as she looked out her window. "I promise not to maul you," she added softly.

He was a screw-up in more ways than one.

But his knee couldn't bear his weight at this awkward angle for much longer.

"Why don't we switch places?" he suggested.

It was even more awkward to try not to brush up against her in the confined space, with the truck at an angle and nothing solid to grab onto except the steering wheel. Finally, he managed to get his tookus in the passenger seat. She perched awkwardly on his thigh, bracing herself against the dash to try and hold herself away from him.

This wasn't gonna work.

He slid his arm around her waist and dragged her into a seated position across his lap.

"We'll be warmer this way," he mumbled.

Even though she hadn't protested.

Having her this close was torture as his mind threw him memories of her kisses, her taste.

He needed a distraction.

"What about Howie," he said in a slightly-strangled voice. "You promised to tell me what happened."

She shrugged, her shoulder nudging his pec. "He was interested. I wasn't. He pushed. I said no."

On his knee, his hand tightened to his fist even though he hadn't consciously made the thought. "What does that mean, *he pushed*?" Had the jerk touched her?

"He got a little forceful with his invitation. So I got a little forceful with my no. I broke his nose."

That was something, at least. Maverick wanted to do much worse.

"Why didn't you tell Cash?"

"I did. And the police. He said it was a mistake, and I dropped the charges. He hasn't bothered me since."

He wracked his adrenaline-slow brain to the conversation they'd been having before the crash. She hadn't outright said she hadn't told Cash. Just let him assume.

So she could quiz him about his knee.

And then ask him why he hadn't *come home*.

That thought was too dangerous to explore.

She was warm and sleepy, her head lolling against his shoulder now.

If he didn't keep her talking, he was going to do something he'd regret—like kiss her again.

"Are you sure that holding on to the ranch is what you really want to do?"

She'd been settling in against him, but now he felt her go completely still. "Why do you think I can't manage it myself?"

"I didn't say that."

She shifted, putting an elbow in his gut, making him "oof!"

"Sorry." He wasn't sure she meant it.

"You've said it several times tonight," she said softly.

He wished he could see her face.

"You didn't think I could take care of my neighbor in the ballroom. Didn't think I could drive down to the barn in a snowstorm."

"*I* drove off the road," he pointed out.

She didn't respond, only stared to the distance.

He was botching this. "Look... do you really think your parents would want you to throw away your plans to be a vet just to run the ranch?"

She shifted slightly, turned her head so he had a clear view of her eyes. "Is that what you think?" She touched his forearm, let her head rest on his shoulder. "Maverick, the whole reason I was going to vet school was to bring that learning back to the Double Cross. I thought about just getting an ag degree, but Dad pushed me to do vet school."

His chin brushed her hair. "Really?"

"Really. The Double Cross is more than

where I live, more than just the family business. The Double Cross is home."

MALLORY WAS close enough to feel the fine tension radiating off Maverick.

The Double Cross isn't my home.

Where was Maverick's home?

What would it be like to feel moorless, no place anchoring you?

Thick clumps of snow barraged the truck, insulating them in a white blanket. The windshield was already almost covered.

She could've made it back home. Even under a foot of snow, she knew every inch of the ranch. It was a part of her.

But she also wanted to stay here with Maverick. Pretend he wanted to take care of her.

This might be her last chance to be this close to Maverick. He'd been clear that he didn't want anything—any kind of relationship—between them.

It can't happen again. No more kissing.

The hope she'd carried until tonight had fractured. She'd thought that the chemistry, the history between them meant something. Had been something he would want.

When he'd held her, the fervor of his kisses... She'd been so sure she was right.

This was the man who as a kid had always made sure she got the last brownie off the plate.

Even now, the way he'd settled her close, was keeping her warm.

It didn't feel like *nothing*.

What if...?

What if he was afraid? He'd lived through a difficult childhood. Had survived a cruel father, an absent mother. His career with the military took him all over the world and put him in dangerous situations. Were his walls up to protect himself?

She'd never forgive herself if she didn't try.

But at the party earlier she'd tried a direct approach and had been shot down. In the barn, emotion had overtaken them both.

She needed a soft touch. The kind Mom had had.

His arm surrounded her body, his hand resting on his thigh. Slowly, she reached out and slid her hand beneath his. She waited for him to pull away, waited for a sigh that might mean he was humoring her.

But all she felt in his body was tension. He was strung tight as a wire.

So she linked their fingers.

And his fingers closed around hers.

She barely breathed, desperately not wanting to scare him off.

"Thank you for helping with Prince tonight," she said.

She felt the movement of his chest when he half-laughed.

"Yeah, you're welcome for getting you stranded in the snow."

"Don't," she said softly. "You made a difference. Prince recognized you. Maybe he fought to get to his feet because he didn't want to disappoint you."

His chin pressed against the top of her head. Or... had he pressed a kiss there?

"You always did think the horses could talk to you."

"They do." Maybe not with words, but even so. "Besides, we both know that if we were in real danger, you'd have figured out some way to get me home. You've got some plan cooking right now in case Cash doesn't show up in the next half hour."

He didn't answer that. He didn't have to. His thumb rubbed the outside of her hand in a slow movement.

She loved this man.

She'd been couching it in safe words. Chemistry. Attraction. Relationship.

But Maverick was one of the good ones. She'd been in love with him for years. It was why no one else could measure up.

And he deserved to know.

She turned her face up toward his.

"Maverick," she started.

But he cupped her jaw with his big hand. He shifted slightly, and she turned toward him.

His lips closed over hers.

His kiss was sweet, gentle.

Not lost in emotion, like the ones they'd shared in the barn.

Their hands were still clasped, and she allowed her opposite hand to and twine into the back of his hair.

She opened to him, wanting him to know everything she felt for him. And he didn't push her away. If anything, he held her closer. *Oh, Mav.*

Too quickly, he pulled back, brushing a gentle kiss against her temple.

She pressed her cheek against his chest, satisfied that his heart was pounding just as hard as hers was.

He hadn't let go of her hand.

She gathered up every piece of courage, the scattered remnants that had been obliterated by him pushing her away earlier in the evening —twice.

"Mav." She cleared her throat because her voice was so husky.

He squeezed her hand.

"I do have a Christmas gift for you."

He shook his head, his chin brushing her brow.

She needed to see his face when she spoke these words.

She shifted from his lap until she rested awkwardly on her knees next to him on the bench seat. She still had to lean against his shoulder for balance.

"You belong here on the Double Cross."

She saw the way his eyes darkened, the denial that sparked there, and rushed on.

"Isn't this where you buried that time capsule when you were eleven?"

He opened his mouth as if he might deny it, then snapped it closed again.

"Where you got dressed for prom?"

"The only reason I went to prom was because your brother dragged me."

She shrugged one shoulder. "What about where you learned to ride? Learned to bake cookies with my mom?"

His eyes had hardened, gone distant again, and he turned his chin slightly away, staring at the white windshield. A muscle jumped in his jaw.

"The Double Cross *is* your home," she finished quietly.

He bared his teeth. Looked at her finally, his eyes flashing. "I don't have a home."

What a sad thing to believe. *"Do you want one?"* The question formed on her lips. But he wasn't done.

"What do you think, that I'm going to come back during my occasional leave? Are you going to spend your whole life waiting on me? You think I won't find someone a little more interesting than a farm girl?"

That was a cruel hit and he knew it. She couldn't help the tears that pricked her eyes.

But she also knew how much he'd been hurt in his childhood, how thick his shields must be.

"You don't have to be Maverick any more, you know," she said softly. "You could just be Sam. Because you belong here." *With me.*

In the face of his defiant denial, she couldn't quite get the words out.

And before she could gather the tatters of her courage again to make an even bigger declaration, bright lights swung over the windshield in an arc.

Cash had arrived.

CHAPTER 7

CASH'S DODGE RAM 3500 WAS A QUAD CAB, which meant that after Maverick tucked her in the passenger seat, he climbed in the back with ease.

Cash was distracted and edgy, still in his tuxedo, with a heavy coat thrown over it and his Stetson low. After he assured himself they both were all right, he didn't say much more.

It only took minutes to reach the ranch house. It was empty, the ballroom dim and quiet, the Christmas tree dark. The catering staff had done a quick clean of the kitchen.

By the time she'd taken a quick look at the iPad to check on Prince, Maverick had disappeared. She hadn't even had a chance to say goodbye.

Cash followed her as she padded among the rooms on the first floor. Her brother was quiet and lost in thought. They moved into the ballroom.

"Are you really all right?" he asked.

She looked at him, her older brother, her beloved brother. She couldn't help seeing Dad in his weary smile, the tiny lines at the corner of his eyes.

Tears welled. "I miss them," she admitted.

Mom would've known how to reach Maverick. She was the best at relationship advice. And if he'd still pushed her away, Mom would have wrapped an arm around Mallory's shoulders and comforted her with homemade ice cream.

Cash's arm came around her shoulders, and he tucked her in for a hug.

"I do, too," he whispered.

He held her for a long time in the shadow of the tree, the scent of fir permeating the air.

When he moved back, he ran a hand through his hair. "I could use some advice," he said. "I messed up. Big time."

She couldn't remember Cash ever asking for advice. And she felt fried, weepy.

"Can it wait for tomorrow?" she asked.

He blew out a blustery sigh. "Yeah. Yeah, it can. You gonna go up and get some rest?"

She nodded. "In a minute."

He bussed a kiss against her cheek and left her. She hoped he was going to catch up with Maverick before the other man left. Maverick needed his best friend, needed to know Cash would always be there for him, even if *there* meant in Austin and not on the Double Cross.

She walked a slow circle around the tree, letting one hand touch the ends of several prickly boughs.

She should go up to bed. But there was a part of her that knew that once she closed her eyes, the Christmas magic would be over.

She hadn't won Maverick's heart. She could only hope she'd touched him, a little.

She felt empty. Raw.

She'd wake up tomorrow morning and spend a quiet Christmas with Cash. Do her chores, check on Prince. Then the next day, it was back to work. Check the herd in the west pasture, follow up with the assayer about the land dispute.

And Maverick would be gone. En route to his next assignment with the Marines.

And Mom wasn't here any longer to send the care packages he'd loved.

But Mallory could.

And maybe, every time he opened one, he'd know that she hadn't forgotten about him. That she still loved him.

She might not have the chance to tell him in person very often, but she could find a way to keep saying it.

The Christmas magic might be almost spent, but Mom would say she should make her own magic.

So she would.

She didn't want to miss her chance to say goodbye. Probably, he'd come downstairs after saying goodbye to Cash.

From the ballroom, she had a decent view of the stairway, the front hall, and the kitchen and its mudroom exit.

She detoured to the living room and took an afghan off the back of the couch, then returned to curl up on the floor near the Christmas tree.

She'd send her soldier off with a goodbye he wouldn't soon forget.

MAVERICK HID in the ranch house's office. It used to be Cash's dad's domain, but he could see Mallory's touches everywhere, just like in the barn.

Ignoring the potted Christmas tree on this huge mahogany desk, he saw some kind of violet flower on the windowsill and a rag rug on the wood floor that he didn't remember. Several framed pictures of her parents and the family throughout the years had been added to make one whole wall a huge collage.

It screamed *Mallory*. The Mallory who would fight fiercely for this place, like she did for everything she cared about.

He shoved his hands in his pockets and perused the photos.

He really needed to get going if he was going to make his flight out of Austin at oh-dark-thirty.

But something held him back. An invisible tether, one that connected him to Mallory, whether he wanted it or not.

Wanting wasn't the problem. He ached for her.

You don't have to be Maverick any more. You could just be Sam.

Recalling her words made the ache worse, the one deep down in his soul where he'd hid away the things he'd really wanted as a child. A house that didn't freeze inside in the winter or roast in the summer. A dad who didn't get drunk and hit him. A wife. Kids of his own.

For so long, he'd been *Maverick*. Not only the name, but the noun. A loner. Wild card. On his own.

Cash appeared in the open doorway. "Good, you're still here."

Maverick couldn't help a small wince. Had Mallory confessed everything? The kisses?

If Cash wanted to knock him out, he wouldn't defend himself. He deserved what the other man would throw.

But Cash didn't come in the room, didn't seem to be spoiling for a fight.

"What time is your flight?" he asked instead.

"Early," Maverick said. Time was short. Too short.

"The roads are a mess, with all the snow and ice. It's supposed to melt off later."

Maverick shrugged. "My truck can handle it."

Cash stepped forward, holding out something

white. An envelope. "Mallory left this on the kitchen counter. It has your name on it."

I really did get you a Christmas gift.

He took it, batted it against his thigh as thick emotion clogged his throat.

"I kissed Mallory," he blurted.

Winced again.

Braced for a punch.

But Cash only looked slightly surprised. "Took you long enough."

He jerked. "What?"

Cash moved forward but only used his fist to nudge Maverick's shoulder. "It's been a long time coming."

Maverick rocked back on his heels. "What's that supposed to mean?"

"She's had a thing for you since high school. And unless I'm totally blind, you've had one for her for nearly as long."

Denial sprang instantly to his lips, but Maverick couldn't quite say the words.

Because he wasn't sure they were true anymore.

He wasn't sure of anything anymore.

"Remember that time—we must've been

sixteen—when we were supposed to go to the movies?"

They'd gone fishing instead, the three of them. The fish weren't biting.

Cash had fallen asleep on the picnic blanket—or so Maverick had thought—and he and Mallory had spent over an hour just talking, their lines and bobbers practically forgotten in the farm pond.

Cash had known. Even back then.

Maverick cleared his throat. "I thought you'd be angry. Tell me to stay away from her."

Cash exhaled noisily, laughing a little. It sounded self-deprecating. "I kissed someone tonight too."

Whoa. Cash ran one hand down his face, his eyes a little wild. "I really liked this girl, and I blew it."

Whoa again.

Maverick was usually the impulsive one, not Cash. He was discombobulated by this woman, whoever she was. Cash was normally even-tempered and worked from a plan.

"Who am I to tell you that Mallory's off-limits? She's a grown woman."

"So she keeps saying," Maverick mumbled.

Then, a little angry, "You know about my background. Mallory deserves somebody so much better than me."

Cash straightened to his full height. "You're my best friend, Mav. You're one of the best soldiers out there."

"Yeah, but look at what I came from—"

"Do you really think I would've been best friends with a piece of trash? Sure, your trailer was. Sure, your dad was. But not you. You were loyal, and strong, and courageous—"

"Yeah, real courageous to come to you crying when my old man beat me up."

He'd never said anything like that aloud. Never admitted what his pops had done to him to anyone else, though Cash had always known.

"You came here because you knew it was safe."

Cash reached for him, and Maverick met him in a quick brother-hug. They moved back quickly and Maverick wiped beneath his eyes, just in case.

"Open that before you go." Cash pointed to the envelope still clutched in his hand. "And stay safe." He left the room.

Maverick sat in Mallory's chair, fingering the

envelope.

She'd said she had a gift for him. It might be a letter. A gift certificate. Something else.

It was already going to be hard enough to leave. Maybe he should wait to open it.

But he slid his thumb under the flap and ripped into the envelope.

It was a plane ticket. Rather, a voucher for a plane ticket, in his name. To be used at any time in the future.

She'd stuck a sticky note to the front of it.

For next time you have leave, she'd written. *Come home.*

He could still hear her, the word she'd spoken in the passenger seat of the truck. *The Double Cross is your home.*

He'd denied it. Tonight and for a long time.

Because he was afraid?

Afraid that if Mallory knew the real him, she wouldn't feel the same way.

That he wasn't worthy of her.

That if he let himself find a place here, start to belong, it would get ripped away from him.

But was that any way to live?

You could just be Sam.

Was that even possible anymore?

CHAPTER 8

SAM STOOD IN FRONT OF THE OPEN FRIDGE IN THE Trudeau's super-fancy kitchen. He had a Saran-wrapped hunk of cheddar cheese in his hand when he heard footsteps behind him.

"Cash, the movie starts in an hour, get a move on!" That was Mrs. Trudeau's voice, calling upstairs. Sounded like she was on her way in here.

He shut the door and whirled around, hiding the cheese behind his back.

He didn't know why Cash Trudeau had decided to befriend him, but he wasn't leaving here empty-handed, not after Dad had agreed to let him come over after school.

Cash was the most popular kid in third grade. He never struggled with the reading or math assignments like Sam did.

And two weeks ago, he'd come to Sam's empty lunch table in the cafeteria and sat next to him.

Sam had bristled, sure he was the butt of some joke, but Cash had started talking about his favorite football team as Sam shoveled food into his mouth as fast as he could.

And Cash sat next to him again the next day.

Sam couldn't figure out why. But he wasn't going to look a gift horse in the mouth. He'd heard his old-lady teacher say that once.

Mrs. Trudeau came into the kitchen and reached for her purse on the counter. "Oh, Sam. What're you doing in here?"

"I was thirsty. I got a glass of water." Stupid. Why did he choose that lie? She'd see that there wasn't an empty glass out. Dummy.

His stomach gurgled. He felt like his stomach was eating itself from the inside. When he'd opened his tin lunch box today, there'd been nothing inside it. He'd ditched the lunch period, because he hadn't wanted Cash to know he had a loser for a dad.

He edged away. If he could just make it into the living room, he could stuff the cheese inside his shirt.

But Mrs. Trudeau cut him off. "What've you got there?"

"Nothing." He was careful to keep any hint of

defiance out of his voice. He already knew he didn't belong in the spotless mansion. He didn't want her to figure it out just yet.

"Sam—"

The back door opened, there was movement in the mudroom, and Cash's dad strode inside. He caught sight of them and drew up short. "Problem?"

Sam froze. Mr. Trudeau was even taller than his dad. He had muscles from working with the ranch animals. If he struck, it would hurt even worse than when Sam's dad hit him.

Heat flamed into Sam's face. Should he run? Maybe he was fast enough to get past Cash's dad and make it outside.

But then he'd have to walk the twelve miles to his house in town.

There was nothing for it. He brought his hand from behind his back, revealing the hunk of cheese to Mrs. Trudeau. He turned his head slightly, because a strike would hurt less if it glanced off his cheek. Or maybe she'd cuff his ear. He braced for the hit.

And jumped when Mrs. Trudeau's hand landed on his shoulder.

"Sam and I were just making a snack before the movie. Wasn't that a good idea?" she said. "If the boys

eat a snack here, they might not want as much junk food at the theater."

He dared to glance at her, knew his eyes were wide. She was going to buy the expensive movie theater food? If he'd known that, he wouldn't have tried to steal the cheese.

She winked at him. Squeezed his shoulder.

"The plates are in that cabinet." She pointed. "Grab two while I slice this up." She ruffled his hair when he turned to obey.

And if his eyes watered a little while he ate the cheese and apples she sliced, she pretended not to notice.

MALLORY WOKE SLOWLY. Her lower back ached, and her elbow was pressed into a hard surface.

The Cattlemen's Ball.

Christmas Eve.

Curling up on the floor near the dark, decorated tree.

Maverick.

If she kept her eyes closed, she could stay asleep. The magic wouldn't be over.

Maybe she was still dreaming, because she could smell him.

Then came a brush of lips against her cheek.

Oh, it was a *good* dream.

"Mal," dream-Maverick whispered. "Wake up, honey."

She smiled. Her dream guy was using endearments. Perfect.

He brushed kisses over both her eyes. The scruff at his jaw caught in her hair, and his dream-hand smoothed it back.

She couldn't help the tear that slipped from her closed lids and down her cheek.

His thumb gently wiped it away.

"Mal," he whispered again. "You're killing me."

That didn't sound much like something a dream would say. She opened her eyes.

It was still dark, silent, and cold outside the ballroom windows. Maverick—the real Maverick—knelt over her, one shoulder brushing the tree that towered above them.

Maverick was still here.

Heart pounding, she pushed to a seated position, brushed her hair out of her face. She was conscious of how disheveled she was. But it was dark. Maybe he couldn't see her makeup from last night running down her face.

"What time is it?" she asked.

"Early."

He was close, but he didn't reach for her.

He'd touched her in her sleep. Was he... nervous?

She squinted into the darkness, trying to see his face. Wishing for light, even a little bit.

He was still, the stillness giving away what he couldn't say.

So she reached for him.

He pulled her into his arms quickly, as if he'd been waiting for an invitation. He pressed her to his chest tightly, and she felt him trembling.

What was going on?

She threaded one arm around the back of his neck; her other arm was stuck between them, but she didn't want to move away.

"Maverick," she whispered. "Wh—"

He pressed a kiss to her jaw. "You said I could be Sam."

Sam.

She freed her pinned arm and framed his face with both hands, let her thumbs brush against his cheekbones. "Sam."

He bent his head and took her mouth, kissing her thoroughly and sweetly.

"Sam," she murmured when he moved to press kisses across her cheek.

"Mal," he whispered into her ear, pressing his face into her hair. "Mal, I—"

He stopped.

She waited, but he was still trembling, just holding her.

And all she could think of was the boy with walls so high...

"I love you," she whispered into the darkness.

His breath caught. His arms banded around her even tighter. "Mal, I—" She felt him inhale a shaky breath. "I don't believe in magic anymore. Not for me."

She pressed her palm against the back of his neck. "I believe enough for both of us."

He turned his head, seeking her mouth. She met him eagerly, expressing everything she felt for Maverick—for Sam—through her kiss.

He broke the kiss first, pressing his cheek against hers. They were both panting for breath.

"I pushed back my flight. I still have to be on base tomorrow, but..." He took a breath, exhaled against the sensitive skin just beneath her ear. "Can I stay? Today?"

Forever.

She held back the word. It wasn't time yet. Soon.

"Stay," she said, squeezing him closer. "I'll run through morning chores, and then we can scrounge up some breakfast. Maybe watch that Christmas movie you and Cash used to love. The one with the BB gun."

He smiled against her cheek. "Deal."

Then he kissed her again.

CHAPTER 9

I<small>T WAS ALL OF TWENTY DEGREES OUTSIDE, BUT</small> Mallory didn't feel a pinch of cold.

It wasn't because she was safely in the barn, either.

Or the Santa hat she wore.

It was because of the man mucking stalls beside her.

"It's like riding a bike, amiright?" she asked with a grin. Maverick had never shied from chores when he'd visited their home as a teen. Even when she and Cash had begged off, he'd do more than his share.

He threw a look over his shoulder and grunted.

"Hey, I said you could stay up at the house."

She spread clean hay in the stall next to where he worked. The stall he was cleaning was the last one. They were almost done.

Cash had been a no-show this morning, had left a mysterious note on the kitchen table. Something about righting a wrong. Even so, with Sam working side-by-side with her, the chores had gone by in a hurry.

Sam leaned the pitchfork against the stall wall and moved out of the way so she could spread hay in the last stall. "I don't mind chores. There's plenty of them to go around where I'm stationed. At least I'm not the rookie anymore."

She tucked the horse back in its stall, and they moved together to push the wheelbarrow and carry the pitchfork back to their places near the tack room.

"*Not minding* chores and doing something you enjoy are two different things," she chided him gently as they put away the implements.

As she turned back to him, he took her waist in his hands. "I enjoy being with you."

She smiled into the kiss he delivered. Shivered at the delicious feel of his hands spanning her waist. Then his fingers spread wide and his thumb hit the sensitive place just beneath her ribs.

She broke from the kiss, twisted away, laughing.

He wore an innocent look. Until one corner of his mouth lifted in a smile. "Still ticklish, I guess?"

But his smile didn't quite reach all the way to his eyes.

Her giggles faded. "What's wrong?"

"Nothing."

She gave him a look.

"I just… I don't know how to do this."

"What? Have a long-distance girlfriend?"

Silence lengthened.

"Is that our relationship status now?"

Her heart pounded as she looked up into his face. Had she jumped the gun? He hadn't returned her declaration of love this morning.

He hadn't had to. She could see his feelings on his face.

She took her scarf from around her neck and tossed it in a loop over his. Used it to reel him in. "We can take things one day at a time."

"I've only got today," he reminded her.

"Then I guess we'd better make it count."

IN THE RANCH HOUSE KITCHEN, Sam broke two eggs into a mixing bowl.

Mallory sat on the counter next to the stove, her legs swinging, leaning on her hands propped next to her thighs on the marble.

She still wore that stupid Santa hat, the white ball on the point bashing into her cheek every time she moved her head.

She was grinning. And completely in the way as he chopped a pepper for the omelets.

He liked her there.

Girlfriend.

Her casual comment kept ping-ponging through his brain. How easily she'd accepted the next relationship status.

How readily she accepted him.

"You're good at this," she said.

He almost nicked his finger but pretended nothing had happened. "Don't sound so surprised."

She shrugged. "I always imagine you living off takeout. That's what Cash does in Austin."

He used the knife to slide the chopped pepper to one side of the cutting board, then reached for the whole tomato.

"Too expensive. And the food's bad for you."

The knife sliced into the crimson flesh.

"Your mom got me interested," he said, hoping he'd affected a casual tone. It wasn't easy. "I made my very first omelet under her tutelage."

When he paused his chopping and glanced up, Mal's eyes had gone soft and serious. "She loved you."

The punch of grief was hard enough to steal his breath. But he panted through it, concentrating on the tomato until every slice was chopped, until the cinch banding his chest loosened.

Mal tipped her head toward him. "I kind of think she's looking down from heaven and smiling at us right now."

He shook his head with an exasperated smile. Probably her mom was rolling over in her grave. Mrs. Trudeau had witnessed him go through some very unfavorable times.

Girlfriend.

He moved past her to pour the whisked eggs

into the pan, where they sizzled. Detoured to the sink to rinse the mixing bowl.

She had no idea what life with a soldier meant. Of what a long-distance relationship felt like.

When he stepped to go past her in the opposite direction—aiming for the spatula in the drawer—she straightened one leg so that he was blocked.

"What's the password?" she demanded playfully.

He smacked a kiss on the end of her nose.

She smiled. "Wrong."

He couldn't help it. He let both hands slip into her hair. He held her there gently as he plundered her mouth, tasting the sweetness that was all Mallory beyond the coffee she'd drunk when they'd come in from the barn.

He could barely remember his name when he pulled away, much less what he'd been doing.

The sizzle from the stove reminded him. Spatula.

He pointed a finger at her as he moved to retrieve the utensil. "Quit distracting me, Mal-Monster." The childhood nickname slipped out, but she only shook her head, her eyes soft.

He should've known better than to let his defenses down.

"You've got a bee in your saddle blanket. Something's bugging you," she said.

Girlfriend.

He kept his focus on the pan, on flipping one side of the omelet to make a perfect half-moon. *Evade.* "How could anything be wrong?"

She nudged his thigh with one sock foot. "Tell me. Is it because I said the g-word out in the barn? Did I freak you out?"

Mal was too perceptive.

She also knew more about him than anyone else, except maybe Cash.

How was it that she didn't know he wanted so much more?

He just didn't trust that he was allowed to have it.

"I can't call home every day," he dared to voice as he flipped the omelet. Almost done.

He got another nudge from her toes. "You said *call home.*" Without looking, he could tell she was smiling.

He flipped off the stove, moved the pan off the hot burner to the cooler side.

He went to her, let his hands rest on the

counter on each side of her. "Mal, I'm being serious. I won't be here on your birthday. Thanksgiving. Maybe not even next Christmas. What if...?"

"I get tired of waiting around?" she asked.

She always saw through him.

He closed his eyes, squeezing his hands against the cool countertop. She'd made him dare to dream that she could be his. That maybe they did belong together. He couldn't bear the thought of getting a phone call—or email—that said she'd grown tired of him.

Her hands settled on top of his, warm and soft and *there*. That stupid hat brushed his jaw, then her cheek bumped his chin as she placed a kiss beneath his jaw.

A whole body shiver wracked him.

"I've waited years for you to notice me. I'm not giving up on you anytime soon."

He let his arms come around her waist. She clutched his shoulders. Holding him.

He buried his face in her neck.

He wasn't good at this. The touchy-feeling stuff that Mal seemed to need from him. He'd never had a good example—couldn't remember one time that his father had said *I love you* or touched him without the intention of hurting him.

He only knew that he would die if she stopped wanting him. If she changed her mind. If she figured out what he already knew—that he wasn't worth dirt.

Were these crazy feelings love? He thought so.

But he didn't know how to say any of that, so he just held her tighter.

"I know," she whispered. One hand stroked his shoulder.

And because Mallory was her mother's daughter, she probably did know.

HE'D MEANT to drive himself to the airport, but Mallory had insisted on making the drive. She had a good argument about taking his truck back to the ranch for safekeeping during his deployment.

She didn't have to argue very hard.

He wanted her with him for every second of every minute he had left.

In his fatigues with his duffel slung over his shoulder, he had her tucked under his arm as they traversed the airport parking garage. She hadn't listened when he'd asked her to drop him off.

She was snug in place, her arm around his waist, matching his steps.

He'd never imagined he'd have the chance to call Mallory *his*. Never imagined feeling his insides ripped in two because he had to leave her.

His pulse pounded in his temples.

He was acutely aware that she'd made a declaration early this morning beneath the Christmas tree. Her whispered *I love you* had lit him up inside like a huge New York City Christmas tree.

He hadn't said it back.

He wasn't a coward. It was just... His feelings were all jumbled up.

An absent mother and crap father were all he had to go on. The Trudeaus had changed his life, giving him what love they could. But they were gone now, too. Cash wouldn't understand how conflicted he felt inside. Sam was worried that somehow his sordid past would come alive inside him, and he'd hurt Mallory.

She was quiet as they crossed several traffic lanes and passed through a small cluster of passengers. The airport was quiet compared to its usual bustle. No one wanted to travel on Christmas. He'd been glad to plan it that way, but not now.

She stood nearby as he checked in for his flight via a kiosk, walked with him toward the security line. She wouldn't be able to follow him any further.

It was time to say goodbye.

He turned to her, set his carry-on at their feet. Took her hands.

The words were right *there*, trapped behind his breastbone.

And she was looking up at him with her heart in her eyes. "I have something else to give you," she said. Her voice shook slightly.

"Mal, I don't need anything else." She was the best gift he'd ever received.

"I want to." She wiggled one hand until he released it, dug in her front jeans pocket. And came up with... a gold band.

"After Mom and Dad passed, Cash kept Mom's ring," she said softly.

His heart rose to his throat as he guessed what she was going to say next.

"This was Dad's," she whispered.

He held up his empty hand to refuse her. "Mal, I can't…"

Her lips firmed in a way he recognized. She spoke over him. "I'm not going to change my mind. About you. About us."

She pressed the simple gold band into his palm. "I want you to keep this until you're sure about me. You don't have to wear it."

He let go of her other hand to reach up to his neck. He fished his chain and dog tags from beneath his shirt and quickly slipped the ring onto the chain. He wouldn't take it off.

His heart was pounding now, and he took her in his arms. Kissed her until they were both breathless.

Or maybe he was breathless with fear.

He tugged her close to his chest, pressed his cheek against her hair. Closed his eyes.

"I love you," he whispered.

She clung even more tightly to his neck. "I know."

He breathed her in.

"I won't forget," she said.

Neither would he.

FIND out what happens with Sam and Mallory on Christmas Eve one year later... get the bonus story Christmas Ever After.

ALSO BY LACY WILLIAMS

SNOWBOUND IN SAWYER CREEK SERIES
(CONTEMPORARY ROMANCE)

Soldier Under the Mistletoe

The Nanny's Christmas Wish

The Rancher's Unexpected Gift

WILD WYOMING HEART SERIES
(HISTORICAL ROMANCE)

Marrying Miss Marshal

Counterfeit Cowboy

Cowboy Pride

Courted by a Cowboy

TRIPLE H BRIDES SERIES (CONTEMPORARY
ROMANCE)

Kissing Kelsey

Courting Carrie

Stealing Sarah

Keeping Kayla

Melting Megan

COWBOY FAIRYTALES SERIES
(CONTEMPORARY ROMANCE)

Once Upon a Cowboy

Cowboy Charming

The Toad Prince

The Beastly Princess

The Lost Princess

HEART OF OKLAHOMA SERIES
(CONTEMPORARY ROMANCE)

Kissed by a Cowboy

Love Letters from Cowboy

Mistletoe Cowboy

Cowgirl for Keeps

Jingle Bell Cowgirl

Heart of a Cowgirl

3 Days with a Cowboy

Prodigal Cowgirl

Made in the USA
San Bernardino,
CA